HUDSON AREA PLD

W9-ATS-360

DISCARD

Hudson Area Public Library
Hudson, Illinois 61748

#13.96 Kenworthy 10/2004

DISCARD

HarperCollins®, ☂®, HarperFestival®, and Festival Readers™ are trademarks of
HarperCollins Publishers Inc.

Maurice Sendak's Little Bear: Asleep Under the Stars
© 2004 Nelvana
Based on the animated television series *Little Bear* produced by Nelvana.
™Wild Things Productions
Little Bear Characters © 2004 Maurice Sendak
Based on the series of books written by Else Holmelund Minarik and illustrated by Maurice Sendak
Licensed by Nelvana Marketing Inc.
All rights reserved. No part of this book may be used or reproduced in any manner whatsoever without
written permission except in the case of brief quotations embodied in critical articles and reviews. Printed
in the United States of America. For information address HarperCollins Children's Books, a division of
HarperCollins Publishers, 1350 Avenue of Americas, New York, NY 10019.
Library of Congress catalog card number: 2003105509
www.harperchildrens.com

1 2 3 4 5 6 7 8 9 10

❖

First Edition

Asleep Under the Stars

BY ELSE HOLMELUND MINARIK

ILLUSTRATED BY CHRIS HAHNER

HarperFestival®
A Division of HarperCollins Publishers

Hudson Area Public Library
Hudson, Illinois 61748

Father Bear was putting up a tent.

Little Bear was going to camp out.

The moon would be full.

The stars would shine.

It would be a bright, bright night.

Little Bear went to look for his friends.

He found Duck in the pond.

"Duck," said Little Bear,

"I'm camping out tonight.

The moon will be full.

You can come, too."

Duck was happy.

She flapped her wings.

Little Bear said,

"Let's go tell Hen, Cat, and Owl.

They can come, too."

Little Bear and Duck walked off.

They found Hen in her garden.

Little Bear said to Hen,

"We are camping out tonight.

You are invited."

Little Bear, Duck, and Hen went to

look for Cat and Owl.

Cat and Owl were in a little boat.

"Come ashore!" called Little Bear.

Cat and Owl came ashore.

Little Bear said,

"We are all camping out tonight.

There will be a full moon.

And you are invited."

"Good!" said Cat. "I love a full moon."

Owl said, "It will be enchanting."

"What?" asked Hen.

"*Enchanting!*" said Owl.

"Nice," said Cat.

"Oh," said Hen.

"Good-bye, everybody," said Little Bear.

"I'm going home.

I'll see you tonight."

Back home, Father Bear had put up
the tent.

"Now it's ready, Little Bear," he said.

Mother Bear packed a basket of goodies.

She said to Little Bear, "You may want a

midnight snack."

"My friends are all coming,"

said Little Bear.

"Good," said Mother Bear.

"Everyone can have a midnight
snack."

Little Bear laughed.

He said, "A moonlight midnight
snack!"

The sun began to set.

The tent was up.

Little Bear was waiting.

He said, "I hope my friends

come soon."

And there they were—Owl, Duck,

Hen, and Cat.

They had their own pillows.

"Good," said Little Bear.

"I'll get my pillow, too."

He got his pillow—and a blanket.

It was a big blanket.

The sun had set.

And there in the sky was a big,

bright moon.

It was a wonderful moon.

21

"I feel like dancing," said Little Bear.

So did Cat, Owl, Hen, and Duck.

They danced in the moonlight.

Around and around they went.

Little Bear and his friends

grew sleepy.

So they went to bed in the tent.

The blanket covered them all.

They were all sound asleep when—

Crash!

The tent shook.

Hen cried *"Eek!"*

Duck hid her head under the blanket.

What could it be?

"Let's go see," said Little Bear.

So they all peeked outside, very carefully.

Something big was on the ground

by the side of the tent.

It had feathers.

It croaked, "I'm hurt! I'm hurt!"

"No, you're not," said Owl.

Little Bear said, "I'll help you up."

He gave the bundle of feathers a lift.

He said, "Up, up, up! There you go!"

The feathery bundle was on its
feet.

"Well, well, well!" said Owl.

"You're a turkey!"

"Yes, I am," said the bundle.

"You hit our tent," said Little Bear.

"I was running," said Turkey.

"Something made a noise in the woods.

So I shut my eyes and ran."

Duck said, "I would have done that, too."

"Turkey," said Little Bear, "we are
going to have a midnight snack.
Please come into our tent."

It was a tight squeeze—but very
nice indeed.

Soon morning came.

Mother Bear and Father Bear
met Turkey.

Turkey said, "I'm a lucky bird."

And so she was.